Doll Baby

Doll Baby

BY EVE BUNTING

illustrated by
CATHERINE STOCK

Clarion Books
NEW YORK

Clarion Books
a Houghton Mifflin Company imprint
215 Park Avenue South, New York, NY 10003
Text copyright © 2000 by Eve Bunting
Illustrations copyright © 2000 by Catherine Stock

Type is 17-point Mrs. Eaves Roman.
Illustrations are executed in watercolor and pencil.
Book design by Carol Goldenberg.

Printed in Singapore.

Library of Congress Cataloging-in-Publication Data

Bunting, Eve, 1928–
Doll baby / Eve Bunting ; illustrated by Catherine Stock.
p.   cm. Summary: A fifteen-year-old girl who is pregnant decides
she wants to keep her baby, not realizing how much harder it will be than
caring for her beloved Daisy Doll.
ISBN 0-395-93094-4
[1. Unmarried mothers—Fiction. 2. Pregnancy—Fiction. 3. Babies—
Fiction.] I. Stock, Catherine, ill. II. Title.
PZ7+ [Fic]—dc21 99-057808 CIP AC

TWP   10 9 8 7 6 5 4 3 2 1

To my grandchildren, with love
—E.B.

. . . .

To Daria
—C.S.

WHEN I WAS LITTLE, I HAD A DOLL.
Her name was Daisy.
I loved to dress her and give her a
bottle.

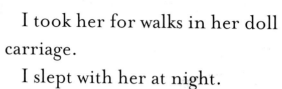

I took her for walks in her doll
carriage.

I slept with her at night.

One day my aunt Jenny asked,
"And where is Daisy Doll's daddy?"

"He's gone away," I said.

Now I go to Grant High and I have a
real baby.

Her name is Angelica.

I love to dress her and give her a
bottle. But because of school it's mostly
my mom who takes care of her.

Aunt Jenny never asked me where
Angelica's daddy is. My mom and my
dad, who is really my stepdad, did,
though. I'll never forget that scary day
I told them I was pregnant.

My mom put her hands over her face. "Oh, no," she moaned. "No." Then she looked at me. "Are you sure, Ellie? How do you know for sure?"

"I know. I missed . . ." My lips were stiff. "I went to the clinic. They told me the baby's nine weeks along."

Mom closed her eyes as if they hurt and Dad put his arms around her. Nobody put their arms around me.

"That free clinic?" Dad asked and I nodded.

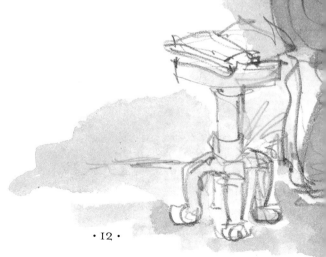

No need to tell them how terrible
it had been. Me there on my own.
Everyone in the waiting room staring.
Maybe they weren't staring, but that's
how it felt. The doctor was nice, though.
And the nurse, too.

"Is it that Hendrix boy?" Dad asked.

I didn't say anything.

"I'll break his neck," Dad said.

Mom began to cry and Dad stroked her hair. I was sniffling, too. It was awful, standing there, the clock ticking so loudly, my heart thumping, Mom and Dad with each other and me by myself. (It's like that a lot since he and Mom met and got married.)

After a minute Mom said, "You know you can't keep it, Ellie. You're just a child yourself." Her voice was softer.

"I'm keeping her," I said. "And I'll love her a lot." I rubbed at my tears.

"But, sweetheart." Mom came close and took my hands. "Think about it. Think about how it would change your life."

"I don't care."

Mom gave me a tissue from her pocket and I blew hard.

"Have you told the . . . the father?" I could tell she was having trouble saying the word or even thinking it.

I nodded.

He'd stood there by the lockers, his eyes shifting from side to side as if he were trapped, and then he'd asked, "How do you know it's mine?"

That hurt so much. This was Charlie, who'd told me he loved me. Who'd said we'd be together always. I could hardly look at him.

"Of course it's yours," I'd said.

He'd given this hard, mean laugh. "That's what you say."

"He doesn't want it," I told my mom.

Dad's fists clenched. "I'm going to have a talk with that jerk!"

"Please! Please don't!" I begged.

Mom pulled me close. "Oh, Ellie! You can't do this! You have no idea how hard it is, taking care of a baby."

"It'll be okay," I said.

There were more days and nights of pleading.

There were long, long months.

Sometimes I didn't feel well and I had to stay home from school. I missed formatting in computer lab and I don't think I'll ever really understand it. I missed the day the woman from the county high school came to speak at assembly. I had wanted to apply to that school for next year. They're into theater and music. I can still try. But maybe . . . maybe I won't be able to go anyway, with the baby and all.

I got fatter and fatter. Even my fingers got fatter. I couldn't wear my birthday ring with the garnets anymore.

My mom's friend Cynthia sent me
a stroller and the baby clothes her
daughter had used for *her* baby. I wished
I could have new, pretty ones instead.
But everything was so expensive. And
Mom and I still had to shop for a lot of
stuff.

I knew we were using the money she
and Dad had put away for their vacation
trip. "No way we can go to the river

this year," Dad grouched when we came home.

Mom spread her hands and gave him a helpless look.

Charlie Hendrix's parents sent him to live with his grandmother in Sacramento. I'm sure it was because they knew about the baby. Good-bye, Charlie. "Where's Daddy?" "Daddy's gone away."

Nothing was easy.

But the first time I felt the baby move inside of me, my very own baby, it was so exciting and mysterious and secret that I had to smile. After that, no matter where I was, even in class, when my baby moved, I'd just smile.

Sometimes I'd sit at my desk and daydream about her, about holding her, snuggling her against me.

I'd dream.

And now the dream is real.

I have Angelica.

Giving birth to her hurt more than I could imagine, even though Mom stayed with me. Even though she coached me the way we'd learned in class. I never thought it would be that bad.

But when I saw Angelica, touched her for the first time, I let go of the pain. I thought my heart would explode with love. My little angel.

I've learned something, though. A baby is not a doll. Angelica is not Daisy.

Taking care of her is hard.

I thought that once she was born things would be pretty much as they were before, only better. But it's not like that.

I can't do stuff anymore.

I can't stay after school for chorus. I have to go home to take care of Angelica. I can't play on the softball team. Betty Galdone's got my position as shortstop. She made all-star.

I took Angelica to the final game, but watching made me sad. I'm not sure why, because Angelica means more to me than being all-star, and I can't blame her. None of this is her fault. But still. I never seem to get a break.

My friends think Angelica is so cute. They call her Jelly Baby and beg to hold her. But they don't want her around all the time. So I don't go out much.

The boys whisper about me. I know they do, but I pretend not to care. Brady McGinnis is nice, though. He sometimes sits with me at lunch, and one day he said, "It's got to be tough, being a single mom."

I guess that's what I am. Fifteen years old and a single mom. It *is* tough.

Charlie Hendrix has come back. To school. Not to me. The word is, he was getting in trouble in Sacramento and his grandma couldn't handle it. What kind of trouble, I wonder.

Last Saturday I saw him in a movie line with Cassie Yokai. I had Angelica in her stroller. We walked right past them, and at first I thought Charlie was

going to ignore us. But he hunched up his shoulders and asked, "How's it going, Ellie?" in this fake, cheerful voice.

"Okay," I said, and slowed. Didn't he want to look at our baby? You'd think he'd at least want to see her.

But he turned his back and I walked on.

What a jerk!

What a scuzz!

I hate him.

So why did I wish it was me going into the Rialto? Not with him, of course, but with somebody. Just to be free to date and have fun. That's all. How come I felt so weepy?

At night I feed Angelica and bathe
her and hold her and sing to her. I read
her *Goodnight Moon*. I do her laundry and
get her formula ready for the next day.
Bottle after bottle after bottle.

Mom's changed to the evening shift
at the restaurant, four to twelve. That
way she can be home days with the baby.

There are two other girls at Grant who are pregnant, and there's talk they may start childcare in school. That might make things easier. I'm sorry for those two girls. They have no idea how it's going to be.

Dad helps me at night. He's good with the baby. One night she had colic and he and I had to take turns walking her. Once she ran a fever and he drove us to the emergency room.

Mostly, though, he just sits in his chair watching TV, waiting for Mom to come home. When she does, she's bushed and goes straight to bed.

"You don't have time for me anymore," he tells her.

I know that's true.

"You think it's easy for me?" Mom asks. "You think I like it?"

I want to speak up, to say I'm sorry. But how could that help now?

I do my homework.

I take my shower.

I wash my hair.

It's eleven o'clock and I'm so tired. Seems like I'm always tired.

Angelica is such a good baby. She sleeps in her bassinet beside my bed and Daisy Doll sleeps with me on the other side.

I stroke Angelica's cheek and her tiny hands. I breathe in the smell of her, careful not to wake her because if she wakes up, she sometimes cries and cries. And I have school tomorrow.

Sometimes in the night I cry and cry, too. I hug Daisy Doll and I wonder if I was right to want Angelica, to keep her. That kind of thinking makes me feel worse and I cry some more.

Sometimes in the night I think about running away. But where would I go? And I could never leave the baby.

Sometimes in the night I think how easy it all was when I was little and only had a doll.